Franklin, the Little Bubble

Kids Can Press

FRANKLIN and his friends loved to visit
Aunt T at her Messy Make-It Shop. She always
had fun and exciting things for them to do.
They might paint pictures, splash in water —
or even stomp in mud!

One day, Franklin and his friends were playing outside the shop when something strange happened.

Tiny bubbles started floating their way! A minute later, they heard a shout from inside.

"Oh, no!" Aunt T shouted.

"Aunt T is in trouble," said Franklin. "Come on!"

Inside the shop, a strange machine was blowing bubbles.
"What's going on?" asked Franklin.
"It's the bubble maker I bought for my party tomorrow,"
said Aunt T. "It's going too fast!"

Franklin took a close look at the machine. A bubble landed on his nose and popped! Franklin jumped and accidentally bumped the bubble maker. The machine chugged to a stop.

"Thanks, my Little Bubble," said Aunt T, giving Franklin a hug. "I had better go open some windows to let these bubbles out."

After Aunt T left, Fox and Rabbit made fun of Franklin's new name.

"Fox and I have to go home now," said Rabbit. "Bye, Little Bubble."

"Yeah, bye, Little Bubble," giggled Fox.

Franklin frowned as they walked away.

"I don't think that's funny," Franklin said.

"Those guys are just kidding around," said Snail.

"It isn't just that," said Franklin. "It's Aunt T. She's always calling me strange names."

It wasn't long before Aunt T came back. She scooped up a poster she had made earlier.

"I have to go hang this up to let everyone know about the party," Aunt T said. "I'm having it here at the Messy Make-It Shop."

"Neat!" said Snail.

"See you both at the party tomorrow," said Aunt T, walking toward town.

"I can't wait!" said Snail. "Everybody will be there."

"Oh, no," said Franklin. "Aunt T is sure to call me her Little Bubble. Snail, you have to help me."

"Help you do what?" asked Snail.

"I have an idea, but we have to hurry," said Franklin.

Franklin and Snail followed Aunt T. They watched from the bushes as she hung up the poster.

"We can't take your aunt's poster, Franklin," whispered Snail. "That would be wrong."

"We're not going to. We'll just make sure no one reads it," replied Franklin.

After Aunt T left, Franklin and Snail got some balloons. They stood
in front of the poster so no one could see it.

That night, Franklin felt relieved. No one knew about the party.
And no one would know about his silly nickname.

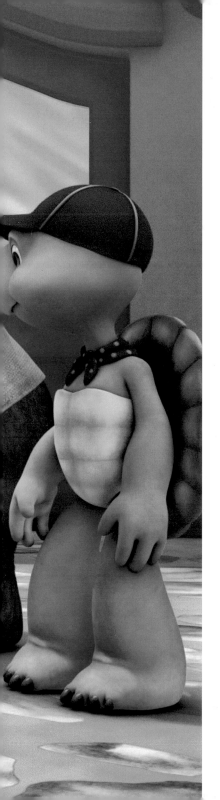

The next day, Aunt T asked Franklin to bring over some paintbrushes. Bear and Snail went with him.

"Hey, my Little Bubble," said Aunt T. "Thanks for bringing the brushes."

Aunt T and Snail took the brushes over to the painting area.

"Did she just call you her Little Bubble?" asked Bear with a chuckle.

"What's so funny about that?" said Franklin, as they wandered over to join Snail.

"It just reminds me of my mom," said Bear. "She always calls me Honey Pot."

"Doesn't it bother you?" asked Franklin.

"No. It just means that Mom cares about me," said Bear.

"I never thought about it that way," said Franklin. That's when he realized that Aunt T's silly nickname wasn't silly at all. It meant that she loved him.

"Uh-oh," said Franklin. "Nobody knows about the party. I have to tell Aunt T."

Franklin found Aunt T inside and told her what he had done.

"Why?" she asked.

"I didn't want anyone to hear you call me Little Bubble. Fox and Rabbit laughed at me," said Franklin. "Are you mad?"

"Of course not," said Aunt T. "I can stop calling you Little Bubble if you want."

"That's okay," said Franklin. "I like being your Little Bubble now."

"Okay then," said Aunt T with a smile. "But how do we get people to come to my party?"

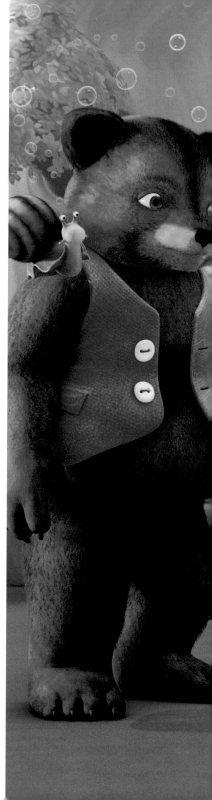

Franklin thought and thought. Then he had an idea.

Aunt T started her bubble machine. She sent bubbles floating into town.

Bear took Snail to see Mrs. Periwinkle, who flew Snail all over town in her little plane. Snail told everyone to follow the bubbles.

Soon the Messy Make-It Shop was full of people. Even Fox and Rabbit came and painted pictures.

"Look, Franklin," said Rabbit, pointing to the sky. "A little bubble, just like you."

Aunt T came by and gave Fox and Rabbit a hug.
"What brilliant pictures, my Little Bubbles," she said to them.
Fox and Rabbit were speechless.
"Don't worry, my Little Bubbles," said Franklin with a laugh.
"It just means that she really cares about you!"